This book belongs to:

....

....

For Dad, from Roo – R.S.

For Gemma and her Oz accent x – L.W.

Editor: Tasha Percy
Designer: Krina Patel
Editorial Director: Victoria Garrard
Art Director: Laura Roberts-Jensen

Copyright © QED Publishing 2015

First published in the UK in 2015 by QED Publishing
A Quarto Group company, The Old Brewery, 6 Blundell Street, London, N7 9BH

www.qed-publishing.co.uk

A catalogue record for this book is available from the British Library.

ISBN 978 1 78171 690 8

Printed in China

What's in Your Pocket?

Ruth Symons & Laura Watkins

QED Publishing

Every day Josh **bounced** around
with the other little joeys.

Every night he **snuggled** into his mum's pouch.

It was a soft, warm pocket of fur – the perfect place to sleep.

When Josh grew bigger Mum told him to
sleep on the grass. But Josh didn't want to.
He tried to climb into her pocket.

"No, Josh," Mum said.
"There's no room."

"Why not?
What's in your pocket?"
Josh asked.

"A surprise – something very special!
Try and guess what it is,"
she said with a smile.

"It's tiny, but it will grow bigger. You can play with it,
but not yet. It needs lots of love and care."

"Will I like it?"
Josh asked the
next morning.

"Of course," Mum said. "You'll love it the minute you see it. It's the most **precious** thing in the world."

Josh couldn't think what it could be, so he went to ask his friends for help.

First, Josh **bounced** up to Katie the koala.

"Hello, Katie," he said.
"Can you help me guess what's in Mum's pocket?
It's **tiny** but will grow bigger. And it's the
most **precious** thing in the world."

Katie scratched
her shaggy ear,

"This eucalyptus tree started
as a **tiny** seed and grew bigger.
Its branches are my home and
its leaves are my dinner!"

"But the most **precious** thing in the world is right here on my back."

Clinging to her back was a cute little koala baby.

"WOW," Josh said. "That **is** precious."

Next, Josh **bounced** up to Peter the parrot.

"Can you help me guess
what's in Mum's pocket?"
Josh asked.

"It's something I can **play** with,
but not yet. And it's the most
precious thing in the world."

"Well, I like to **play** with my friends, and sometimes I **play** the drums on this tree trunk."

"But the most **precious** thing in the world is up there. Look!" Peter said.

Josh looked up at the top of the tree. A tiny parrot face was peering down from its nest.

"WOW," Josh said. "That is precious."

Next, Josh tried Terry the termite. He was
marching around his tidy termite mound.

"Hello, Terry," said Josh. "Can you help
me guess what's in Mum's pocket?

It needs lots of **love** and **care**. And it's
the most **precious** thing in the world."

"My termite mound needs lots
of **love** and **care**," said Terry.

"It's my home, and
I've worked hard to make
it strong and safe."

"But the most **precious** things in the world are the termites inside."

Terry's friends and family all came out to wave at Josh.

"WOW," said Josh. "They **are** precious!"

Josh **bounced** back to Mum.

Whatever was in her pocket, it couldn't be a baby

koala, or a tiny parrot, or a whole family of termites!

"I give up," said Josh.
"What have you got in your pocket?"

"It's your baby brother," said Mum.

A teeny tiny joey poked his head out. He was small, and delicate, and **very precious**.

Josh loved him the minute he saw him.

"WOW!" said Josh.
"That **is** a good surprise!"

NEXT STEPS

Show the children the cover again. Could the children have guessed what the story would be about from just looking at the cover?

Josh can't guess what his mum has in her pocket. What did the children think it would be? Were they surprised at the end of the story?

Ask the children if they have ever been given a surprise. What is the best surprise that they can think of? What do they think is the most precious thing in the world?

Play a simple guessing game in pairs. One child thinks of an animal and gives the other child three clues to guess what it is.

Do any of the children have a baby brother or sister? Do they treat them with lots of love and care?

Do the children recognize any of the animals in the story? Do they know what country they all live in? Can the children think of any other animals that live in Australia?

Talk about kangaroos. A baby kangaroo is called a 'joey'. It lives inside its mum's pouch to keep it warm and safe. It will live there until it is about eight months old.

Ask the children to act out their favourite animal in the story. Can they jump like Josh, play the drums like Peter or march around like Terry?

"But most of all," smiled Mum. "Once you're asleep **we love you**. That's what we do. And we can't wait for more questions in the morning."

"we thread sleep with dreams of icy whiskers, tropical parks and moonlit dancing flight."

We rock the tree boughs to
hush noisy nightingales.
We light the **stars**.
We raise the **moon** . . .

"When dogs bark, we sing soothing lullabies.

If a car goes past, we spread blankets
on the street to silence the wheels.

"it's our job to make sure
everything stays peaceful.

"I wish I could fly," murmured Connor.

Claire yawned and stretched.
"If you're flying,
who's looking after us?"

"We are," said Mum.
"We're always looking
after you."

"Close your eyes,"
whispered Dad.

"Once you're asleep . . .

and we're **flying**! We **loop** the **loop** through the living room. We **twist** and **twirl** in the hall. We **glide** outside and **dance** on the moonlit air.

That's what we do, **once you're asleep."**

"we stand quietly in our slippers, waiting for just the right moment . . .

Very slowly, our heels lift off the floor . . .

"That's silly," laughed Connor. "Everything would be **wet** in the morning!"

"What do you really, really, **really do?**" asked Clare.
"Tell us, or **we won't go to sleep!**"

"My turn," said Mum. "**Once you're asleep . . .**

"That's why we're always so tired."

Course, we have to clean up afterwards, which takes a while . . .

"we drag all the furniture outside,
get the hose on full blast and build

a SPLASHTASTIC TROPICAL WILD WATER DISCO PARK!

That's what we do, once you're asleep . . .

"Okay." Dad spread his hands. **"Once you're asleep . . .**

Connor, Clare and Little Peg hooted with laughter.

"That's cats!" cried Clare.

Connor shook his head.

"You wouldn't fit through the cat flap! Tell us what you really, really do."

We yowl at the moon, rulers of the rooftops and the midnight sky.

That's what we do, once you're asleep."

"we lie next to the cat flap, taking turns to push our noses out.

It's cold!

Fast and free, we slink into the glittering night.
The sky is frosted with stars. The icy air tingles our whiskers.

"Go on, tell us,"
said Clare.

"What do you really do?"

Mum thought for a
moment. Then she said, **"Once you're asleep . . .**

At least, that was the idea.

"What do you do after
we go to sleep?"
asked Connor.

"Do you eat chocolate?"

"Ha!" said Dad.
"There's never any left!"

Connor, Clare and Little Peg did.

They snuggled down tightly so no questions could escape.

"That's enough questions for today," said Mum.

"If you want time for a story?" added Dad.

"How big are tiger teeth?"
asked Clare.
"How are mirrors made?"
called Connor.

"Where Teddy?!"
yelled Little Peg.

Connor, Clare and Little Peg loved ending their day with a pillow fight.

A pillow fight stuffed with questions.

Once You're Asleep

Sarah Coyle

Carolina Rabei

EGMONT

For Mum and Dad
x
S.C.

To Teo, Mihai and Iustin
C.R.

EGMONT
We bring stories to life

First published in Great Britain 2020 by Egmont Books UK Limited
2 Minster Court, London EC3R 7BB
www.egmontbooks.co.uk
Text copyright © Sarah Coyle 2020
Illustrations copyright © Carolina Rabei 2020

Sarah Coyle and Carolina Rabei have asserted their moral rights.

ISBN 978 1 4052 9265 8
70194 /001
Printed in China.

A CIP catalogue record for this title is available from the British Library.

Egmont takes its responsibility to the planet and its inhabitants very seriously.
We aim to use papers from well-managed forests run by responsible suppliers.

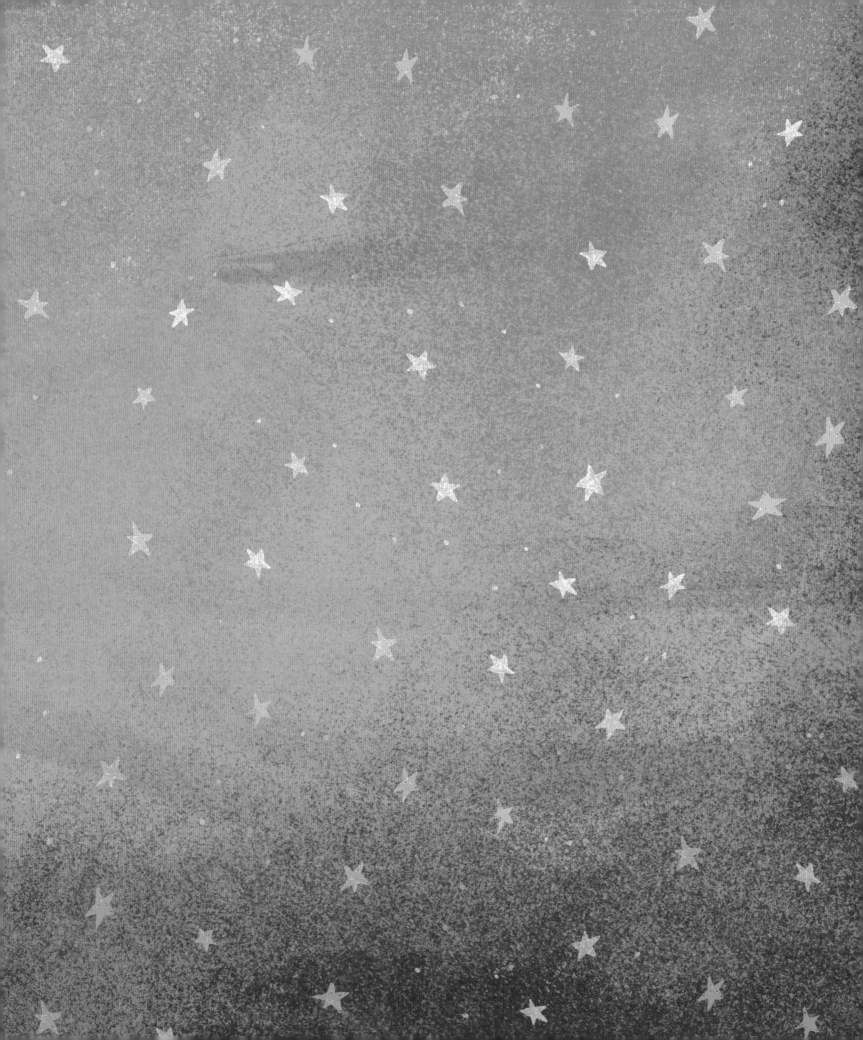